# All about Robots

Happy House

# About Wise & Wide

- A systematic 6-level English reading program based on Lexile® measures
- Diverse and interesting topics chosen from the elementary curriculums of Korea and English speaking western countries
- Well-written books in various forms including fiction stories, descriptive texts, and classics retold
- The informative but original fiction stories grab your interest, leading to the easy and clear understanding of the educational content.
- Improve thinking skills with solid after-reading activities at all levels of the series.

**Wise & Wide** is a 6-level English reading program that consists of 60 books and each level is systematically divided by Lexile® measures. The Lexile® Framework for Reading is the most popular reading measuring system in American formal education curriculums and many English programs. Over 20 out of 50 states in the U.S. mark Lexile® measures directly on students' final report cards and over 300 well-known publishers adopt and use Lexile® measures.

Experience many kinds of readings written by professional writers from the U.S. and England. They used interesting topics that were carefully chosen after analyzing elementary curriculums from around the world including Korea, the U.S., England, and Australia among many others. Comprehensive after-reading activities including graphic organizers, speaking tasks, and After-reading Tests are ready for you.

Levels in the series and their corresponding Lexile® measures

| Level | Lexile® measures | U.S. Grade |
| --- | --- | --- |
| Level 1 | Below 200L | Pre K - K |
| Level 2 | 190L - 400L | Lower Grade 1 |
| Level 3 | 350L - 530L | Upper Grade 1 |
| Level 4 | 420L - 650L | Grade 2 |
| Level 5 | 520L - 940L | Grade 3 - 4 |
| Level 6 | 830L - 1070L | Grade 5 - 6 |

* Smart Readers: Wise & Wide level 1 is applicable to the preschool level in the U.S.

* The source of the relationship between Lexile® measures and U.S. school grades: CCSS(Common Core State Standards) FOR ENGLISH LANGUAGE ARTS, APPENDIX A (2012, which is used by 45 states in the U.S.)

# Topic List

| | Level 1 | Level 2 | Level 3 | Level 4 | Level 5 | Level 6 |
|---|---|---|---|---|---|---|
| **Book 1** | Science>Biology: The hibernation of animals Story | Science>Biology: Living and nonliving things Story | Science>Biology> Animals & the Environment: Sea otters Story | Environment> Living with nature: The diver & the persimmon tree Story | Science>Biology> Animal: Amazing animals of the Amazon Story | Science>Biology: Germs, transmitted diseases Story |
| **Book 2** | Literature> World classics: Aesop's fables Story | Literature> Traditional fairy tale: Old tales about stones Story | Social Studies> Economy: To run a business to make and save money Story | Science>Biology> Plants: Photosynthesis Story | Science>Earth science: Earth's layers,earthquakes, volcanoes, and earth's atmosphere Report | Mathematics> Sequence: The golden ratio & the Fibonacci sequence Story |
| **Book 3** | Science>Physics: How shadows are formed Story | Literature> World classics: Peter Pan Story | Science>Scientific technology: Nanobots Story | Literature>Myths: World's creation stories Story | Literature> Legend: The story of King Arthur Story | Literature>Myths: Constellation myths Story |
| **Book 4** | Literature> Traditional literature: The Talmud Story | Science>Biology> Animal: Polar bears Story | Science>Biology> Animal: Mountain gorillas Story | Social Studies> Cultural anthropology: Amazing ancient cultures of the world Story | Science> Earth science: Clouds and weather Story | Literature> Human & animals: The friendship between a girl and a horse Story |
| **Book 5** | Social Studies> Ethics: Rules in daily life Story | Science>Biology: The five senses Report | Social Studies> Cultural anthropology: Astonishing festivals Report | Art>Music: Stories from two operas Story | Social Studies> World culture & history: The Renaissance Story | |
| **Book 6** | Social Studies> World geography & travel: Tourist attractions around the world Story | Science>Biology> Animal: Dinosaurs Story | Science> Astronomy: The solar system Story | Social Studies> People: Three great people who overcame hardships Story | Science>Scientific technology: The wonderful world of robots Report | |
| **Book 7** | | Social Studies> Cultural anthropology: Mythological monsters from around the world Report | | Science & Social Studies> Technology & culture: Inventions from around the world Report | Art>Works of art: Famous paintings Report | |
| **Book 8** | | | | Social Studies> History: The California Gold Rush Report | Social Studies & Science> Psychology: Psychology in everyday life Story | |
| **Book 9** | | | | | | |
| **Book 10** | | | | | | |

10 books in each level will be published.

# How to Use This Book

## • Before Reading

You can easily find the topic and what kind of story you are about to read.

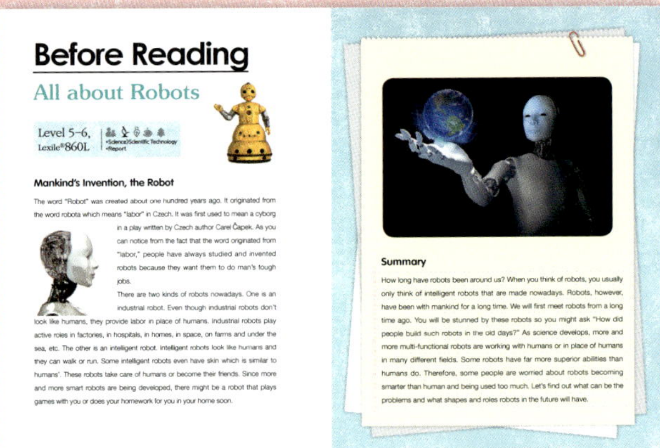

## • The text

All the stories were written by professional writers from the U.S. and England, so you will read authentic and appropriate English sentences and expressions in every book in the series.

## • Pop Quiz

Check out right away if you understand what you have just read by solving a pop quiz that checks your comprehension.

## • Key Words

The key words and expressions on each page are listed for you to easily study them.

## • Aha! Tips

Download free Korean explanations at *www.ihappyhouse.co.kr* for all of the sentences marked with "Aha!". These explain cultural, scientific, and economic knowledge or they deal with aspects of English such as grammatical structures or idiomatic expressions. There are lots of "Aha! Tips" to help you understand the text.

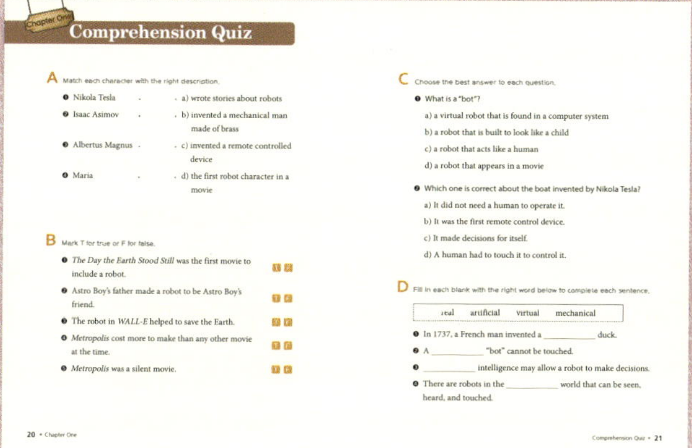

## •Comprehension Quiz

After reading one chapter, solve various questions to find out if you fully understand the content.

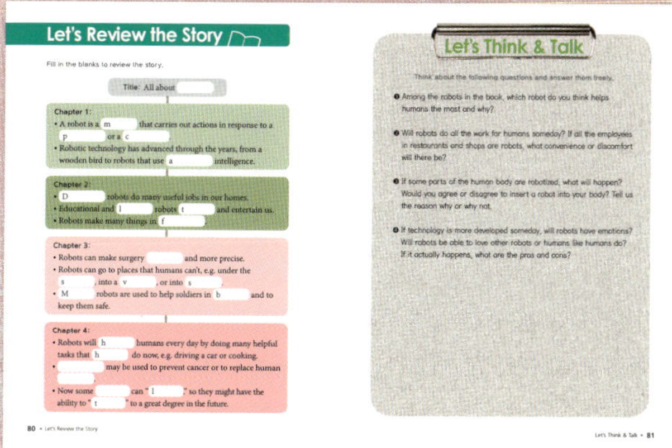

## •Let's Review the Story /
## •Let's Think & Talk

Fill in the blanks in the organizer to summarize the whole story. Express your own thinking and feelings about the story by answering the questions. You can build up logic and reasoning skills for your essay examinations in the future.

## Appendix

### Audio CD

In the CD audio book form, the texts are read vividly by American professional voice actors.

### After-reading Test

Solve an additionally provided After-reading Test for each book.

### The Korean translation, Answer Keys, a Word Quiz, a Word List, and Aha! Tips for each book

You can download them for free at *www.ihappyhouse.co.kr*

# Before Reading

## All about Robots

Level 5–6,
Lexile® 860L

• Science⟩Scientific Technology
• Report

### Mankind's Invention, the Robot

The word "Robot" was created about one hundred years ago. It originated from the word robota which means "labor" in Czech. It was first used to mean a cyborg

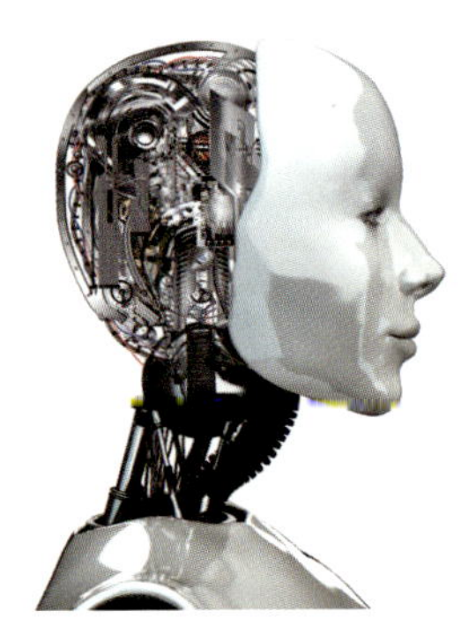

in a play written by Czech author Carel Čapek. As you can notice from the fact that the word originated from "labor," people have always studied and invented robots because they want them to do man's tough jobs.

There are two kinds of robots nowadays. One is an industrial robot. Even though industrial robots don't look like humans, they provide labor in place of humans. Industrial robots play active roles in factories, in hospitals, in homes, in space, on farms and under the sea, etc. The other is an intelligent robot. Intelligent robots look like humans and they can walk or run. Some intelligent robots even have skin which is similar to humans'. These robots take care of humans or become their friends. Since more and more smart robots are being developed, there might be a robot that plays games with you or does your homework for you in your home soon.

## Summary

How long have robots been around us? When you think of robots, you usually only think of intelligent robots that are made nowadays. Robots, however, have been with mankind for a long time. We will first meet robots from a long time ago. You will be stunned by these robots so you might ask "How did people build such robots in the old days?" As science develops, more and more multi-functional robots are working with humans or in place of humans in many different fields. Some robots have far more superior abilities than humans do. Therefore, some people are worried about robots becoming smarter than human and being used too much. Let's find out what can be the problems and what shapes and roles robots in the future will have.

# Contents

# All about Robots

# All about Robots

# The History of Robots

"Most have come to destroy us. Some have come to protect us."
You might recognize this line from one of the *Transformers*
movies. It is talking about robots.

Do you think it is true? Are most robots here to destroy us? Or
will they end up helping and protecting us?

The *Terminator* movies suggest that robots will one day kill all
humans and rule the world!

**KEY WORDS**

- most
- destroy
- some
- protect
- recognize
- end up + *Verb*-ing
- suggest
- rule

The droids or robots in the *Star Wars* movies, however, are helpful and friendly toward humans.

What do you think? Is a robot our enemy or our friend? This question interests many people, and there have been lots of movies about robots.

▲ Maria in the movie *Metropolis*
(By Jiuguang Wang from Pittsburgh, Pennsylvania, United States [CC BY-SA 2.0 (http://creativecommons.org/licenses/ by-sa/2.0)], via Wikimedia Commons)

The first movie to include a robot was called *Metropolis*. It was made in 1926, and featured a female robot called Maria. It was, like other movies of the time, a silent movie. At that time, it was also the most expensive movie ever made!

## KEY WORDS

- **droid** (= android)
- **toward(s)**
- **enemy**
- **interest**
- **lots of** (= a lot of)
- **include**
- **feature**
- **female** (↔ male)
- **silent movie**
- **at that time**
- **expensive**
- **ever**

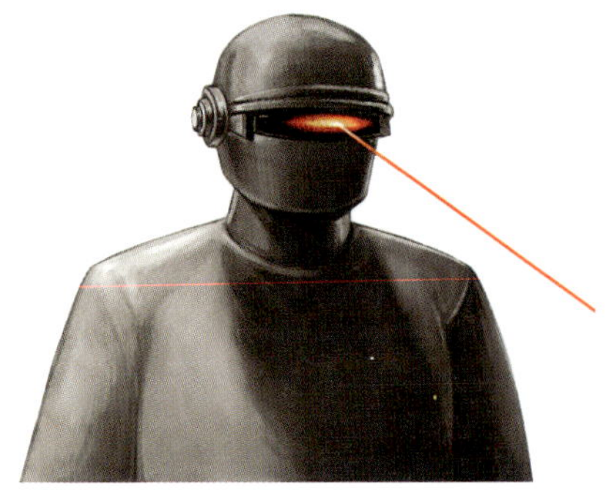

A famous robot movie, *The Day the Earth Stood Still*, was made in 1951. This science fiction story included both aliens and robots! A robot, named Gort, sent out death rays (a bit like lasers) to destroy anyone who threatened it. More recent robot movies include *WALL-E*, a computer animated movie made in 2008. In this movie, a lovable robot helped to save the Earth.

In 2009, *Astro Boy* told the story of a father who tried to make a robot to replace his lost son.

And in 2014, *Earth to Echo* featured an alien robot that needed human friends to help him rebuild his spaceship.

### POP QUIZ

In which movie does a father make a robot to replace his son?

ⓐ Earth to Echo
ⓑ Astro Boy

**KEY WORDS**

- **stand still** (stand-stood-stood)
- **science fiction**
- **alien**
- **send out** (send-sent-sent)
- **death ray**
- **a bit**
- **threaten**
- **recent**

- **animated**
- **lovable**
- **save**
- **replace**
- **lost**
- **rebuild** (rebuild-rebuilt-rebuilt)
- **spaceship**

So what exactly is a robot? Is it something from space or something made on earth? Most movie robots are made of metal, and they can walk and talk like a human. But the real world of robots is far wider than this.

Simply, a robot is a machine that carries out actions in response to a program or a command.

There are also robots (often known as "bots") in the virtual world of computer science. These virtual robots cannot be heard, seen or touched.

In this book, we will look at robots in the real world that can be seen, heard and touched.

In the modern world, robots are usually shaped like humans. But they did not begin that way, nor do they have to be this way.

**KEY WORDS**

- exactly
- space
- be made of
- metal
- simply
- machine
- carry out

- in response to
- command
- virtual
- modern
- not A nor B
- shape

People have always been interested in the idea of objects that can move on their own. In 400 BC, a Greek man invented a bird that could fly. It was made of wood and powered by steam. It could fly 200 m, which is about the same length as eight swimming pools.

Imagine that flying over your head!

Even stranger robots were invented in the 13th century. There is a legend that a man called Albertus Magnus made a mechanical man out of brass. People asked it questions, and the brass man answered. Some people thought that it was magic.

**KEY WORDS**

- be interested in
- object
- on one's own
- **BC** (before Christ)
- Greek
- invent
- be powered by

- century
- length
- legend
- mechanical
- out of
- brass

Magnus used the brass man as a servant in his home.

It is said that the brass man talked so much that one of Magnus'

students became very angry with it. At last, he was so angry

that he smashed the brass man to pieces with a hammer!



**KEY WORDS**

- servant
- smash to pieces (*cf.* piece)

In 1737, a French man invented a mechanical duck. It was able to walk, quack, and flap its wings just like the real thing. People fed it real food, which came out at the other end as poop! The people were amazed because they thought that the duck was able to digest the food that they gave it. In reality, there was a special part inside the duck that was full of poop. This was mechanically pushed out whenever anyone put food into the duck's mouth.

The first remote control device was a boat, invented by Nikola Tesla in 1898. He showed his boat to a crowd in New York. The boat was controlled by radio waves, and signals were sent to it from a special box. The box gave instructions to the boat to make it go forwards, backwards, or to change direction.

## KEY WORDS

- quack
- flap
- real thing
- feed (feed-fed-fed)
- poop
- amazed

- digest
- in reality
- push out
- whenever
- remote control
- device

- radio wave
- instruction
- forward(s) (↔ backwards)
- direction

▲ Isaac Asimov

In 1940, a writer called Isaac Asimov wrote some short stories about a robot which protected a child and seemed to show affection.  He went on to write many more stories about robots, and he was the first person to use the word "robotics," which is still used today.



## KEY WORDS

- seem
- affection
- go on to + *Verb*
- robotics
- phrase
- artificial
- intelligence
- gather

- **UK** (United Kingdom)
- **mean** (mean-meant-meant)
- **normally** (= usually)
- **require**
- **make a decision** (make-made-made)
- **translate A into B**
- **behave**

In 1956 another new phrase, "artificial intelligence," was first used by scientists gathered in the UK.

Artificial intelligence means that a robot can do things that would normally require human intelligence. This may include making decisions or translating one language into another.

At this time, robots began to look and behave more and more like humans!

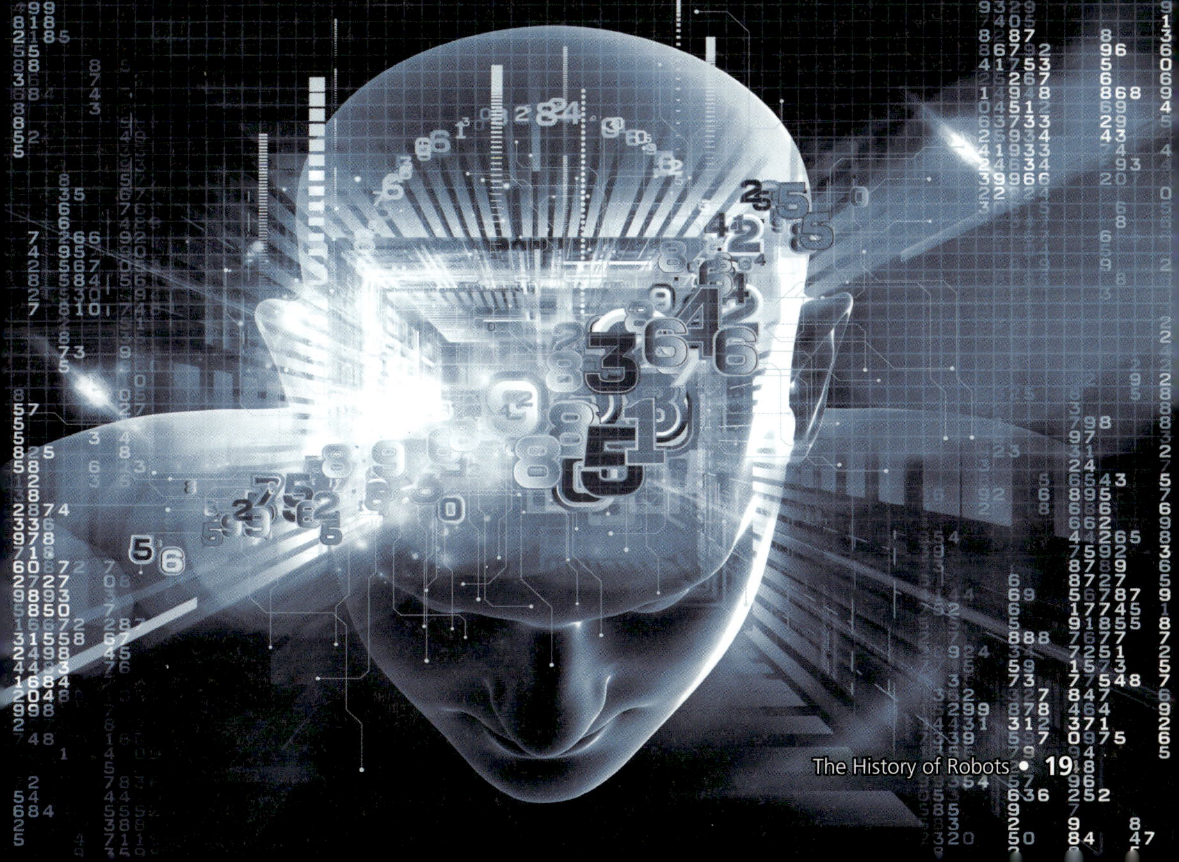

# Comprehension Quiz

**A** Match each character with the right description.

❶ Nikola Tesla   •    • a) wrote stories about robots

❷ Isaac Asimov   •    • b) invented a mechanical man made of brass

❸ Albertus Magnus   •    • c) invented a remote controlled device

❹ Maria   •    • d) the first robot character in a movie

**B** Mark T for true or F for false.

❶ *The Day the Earth Stood Still* was the first movie to include a robot.    T F

❷ Astro Boy's father made a robot to be Astro Boy's friend.    T F

❸ The robot in *WALL-E* helped to save the Earth.    T F

❹ *Metropolis* cost more to make than any other movie at the time.    T F

❺ *Metropolis* was a silent movie.    T F

# C Choose the best answer to each question.

**❶ What is a "bot"?**

a) a virtual robot that is found in a computer system

b) a robot that is built to look like a child

c) a robot that acts like a human

d) a robot that appears in a movie

**❷ Which one is correct about the boat invented by Nikola Tesla?**

a) It did not need a human to operate it.

b) It was the first remote control device.

c) It made decisions for itself.

d) A human had to touch it to control it.

# D Fill in each blank with the right word below to complete each sentence.

| real | artificial | virtual | mechanical |
|------|-----------|---------|-----------|

**❶** In 1737, a French man invented a _____________ duck.

**❷** A _____________ "bot" cannot be touched.

**❸** _____________ intelligence may allow a robot to make decisions.

**❹** There are robots in the _____________ world that can be seen, heard, and touched.

# Chapter Two

# Robots in Everyday Life

Most people don't realize that there are thousands of robots all around them! For example, most kitchens in developed countries contain a microwave oven. Since this is a device that responds to programmed instructions, it is a type of robot. What about a remotely controlled television?

Like Tesla's boat, it receives a signal from your remote control. The TV responds to that signal by changing the channel or the volume. Modern television can record movies or TV programs when no one is home. So they are robots, too.

Coffee makers, dishwashers, washing machines and dryers all respond to programmed commands.

**KEY WORDS**

- for example
- developed
- contain

- microwave oven
- since
- respond

- receive
- record

Many of these domestic robots can tell what time it is and will switch themselves on at the correct time. Others change their actions in response to things that they sense. For example, if the water in a washing machine does not empty, the washing machine will stop and an alarm light will flash. These machines have been in use for a long time. We don't think there is anything unusual or amazing about them.

**KEY WORDS**

- domestic
- switch on
- sense
- empty
- alarm

- flash
- **be in use** (↔ be out of use)
- **unusual** (↔ usual)
- amazing

However, recent technology has produced more unusual and exciting domestic robots. There are robots that will move about and perform difficult or boring tasks.

For example, robots can clean a swimming pool, vacuum the floor or mow the lawn. They can be programmed to operate during certain hours of the day. They respond to the size and shape of their environment. Once programmed, their human owners need not worry about tasks that they find annoying or difficult.

## KEY WORDS

- technology
- **produce** (*cf.* production)
- exciting
- move about
- perform
- boring
- task
- vacuum

- mow
- lawn
- operate
- during
- certain
- environment
- annoying

Sometimes the robot can take the place of a human in other ways. There is the comforting robotic "hug," a pillow programmed to squeeze a person as if someone were hugging them! Or there are baby cradles that rock automatically when the baby cries or moves about too much.



**POP QUIZ**

Mark T for true or F for false.

Robots cannot replace a human in any ways.     T / F

**KEY WORDS**

- sometimes
- take the place of (take-took-taken)
- comforting
- robotic
- hug
- pillow
- squeeze
- cradle
- rock
- automatically

A Japanese robot called Wakamaru
carries out simple tasks about the
house, but it can also act as a
human companion. It can
take care of the house
when the owner is away.
It can even contact a security
company if anyone tries to get in.
It is around 1 meter tall and
recharges its own batteries when
they are running low.



**KEY WORDS**

- companion
- take care of
- be away
- contact
- security

- **get in** (get-got-gotten)
- around
- recharge
- **run low** (run-ran-run)

It is extremely useful for people who have health problems, because it can be programmed to contact a doctor or hospital if something is wrong.

Wakamaru recognizes up to ten thousand words. This means that it can respond to human commands and even hold a conversation.

If you would like one, it will cost you around $14,000!

How many words does Wakamaru recognize?
ⓐ 10,000
ⓑ 14,000

There are smaller companion robots available.

Some robots sit on the desk with their owners and read emails to them. They make the owners feel as if they had one of their good friends with them.

Another useful little robot is the wheelphone robot.  It can bring your cell phone to you, avoiding obstacles on the way. Or you can use it as a home security device.

The wheelphone robot patrols your home. It carries your cell phone, which records pictures or videos.

▲ wheelphone robot

There are many children's toys that use robotics.

Toy cars may be guided by remote control. Others may be guided by technology that uses light to follow a black line made by a marker pen.

**KEY WORDS**

- guide
- follow
- marker pen
- such as
- cuddle
- appear

- popular
- insect
- hit (hit-hit-hit)
- animatronic
- dinosaur
- full-sized

There are dolls and animal toys that respond to actions such as being fed or cuddled. Some of them can speak and appear to hold a conversation.

One popular toy is a robotic insect. It responds to its environment by changing direction whenever it hits a wall. If you have several thousand dollars to spend, you can even buy an animatronic dinosaur! It's full-sized and looks real. Aha!

**POP QUIZ**

**Which is a robotic toy?**

ⓐ a wheelphone robot

ⓑ an animatronic dinosaur

Some robotic toys have a more educational purpose. For example, there are various systems that help children to learn to read.

The child holds a special pen over a word, and a voice reads that word aloud. The child learns how to say it.

Many schools in the UK use "roamers." These are devices that move about on the floor in response to simple computer instructions. In this way, children can learn about distance, directions and angles.

**KEY WORDS**

- educational
- purpose
- hold
- roamer
- distance
- angle

As well as being
helpful at home
and school, robots
have many uses
in factories and
in entertainment.
Many of the things

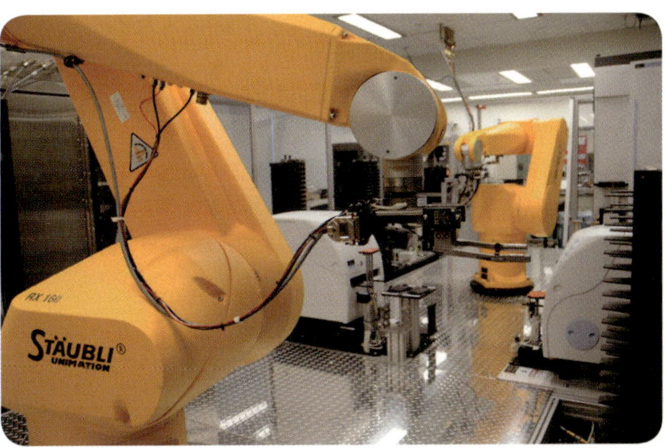

we use in everyday life are made in factories.
Many factories use robots to do the work of building things.
A robotic arm can repeat the same movement over and over
again. It is very precise and never gets tired from long working
hours nor distracted by things around it.
This means that production can go on day and night without
stopping. It is especially useful when making tiny things such as
electronic circuit boards.

## KEY WORDS

- as well as
- have many uses
- entertainment
- build
- repeat
- movement
- over and over again
- precise

- get tired
- distract
- go on
- without + *Verb*-ing
- especially
- tiny
- electronic
- circuit board

Robot arms are commonly used in car factories. They put together the different parts of a car and also paint them. The more robots there are in a factory, the fewer humans are needed to do the work. Aha!

Not all robots stay on the ground.

**KEY WORDS**

- commonly
- put together (put-put-put)
- part
- paint
- ground
- pilotless
- drone
- although
- military
- operation
- film
- bungee jumping
- parachuting

▲ a drone for filming that is flying around an iceberg

There are many pilotless flying robots called drones in use. Although some are used for military operations, others may be used to film movie scenes or other special events. There are some things, such as bungee jumping or parachuting, that can't be filmed from the ground.

A drone can be operated from the ground and the pictures sent back to the operator.

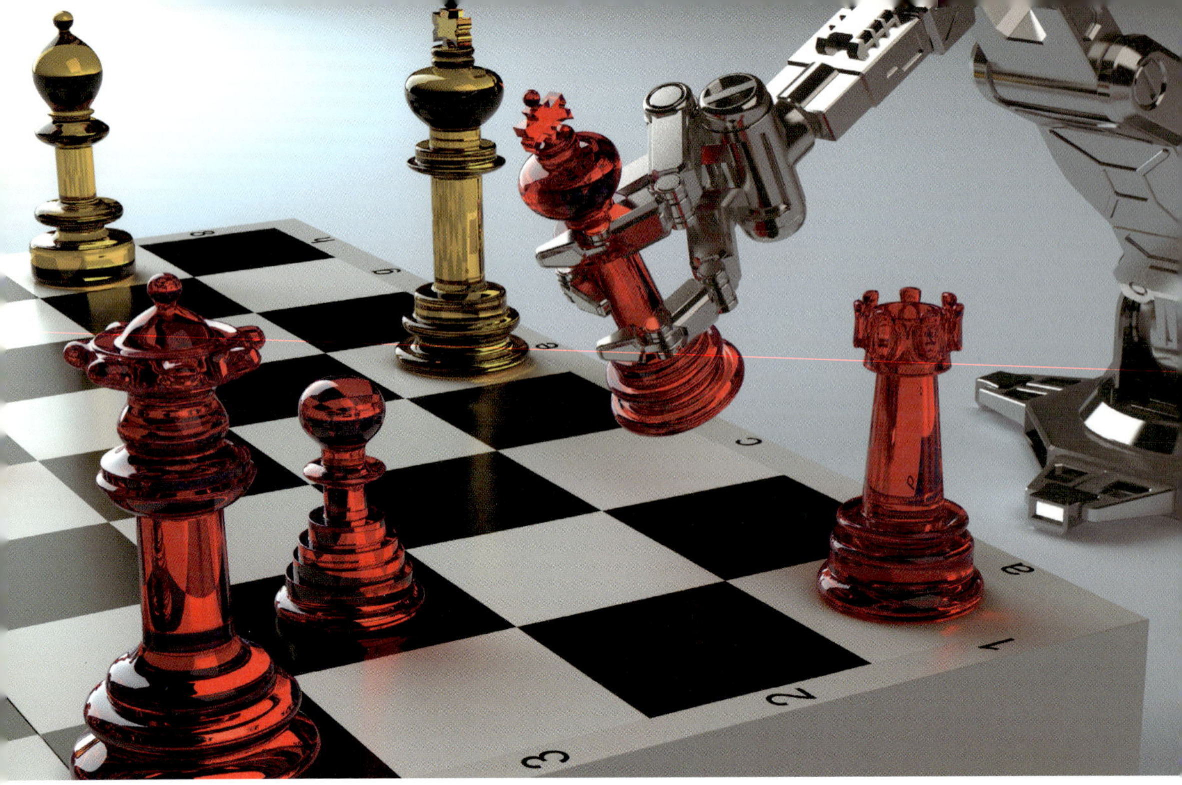

Robots may also be used in leisure and entertainment.

For many years, there have been computer programs that can play chess against a human. But now there is a robot that can actually pick up real chess pieces. It moves them to a different space on the chess board.

Robots can be designed to play golf, to deal cards, or to play table tennis. With skill and imagination, humans can make a robot to do almost anything!

**KEY WORDS**

- leisure
- against
- actually
- pick up
- chess piece
- design
- deal
- table tennis
- skill
- imagination
- afford

Of course, not everyone has robots in their home, their school, or even in their factories. There are many people all over the world who cannot afford to include robots in their everyday life. Recent data have suggested that around 50% of the world's robots are in Asia. About 30% are in Europe and around 16% are in North America. The biggest users of robotic technology are the Japanese.

▼ a chart showing robot distribution around the world

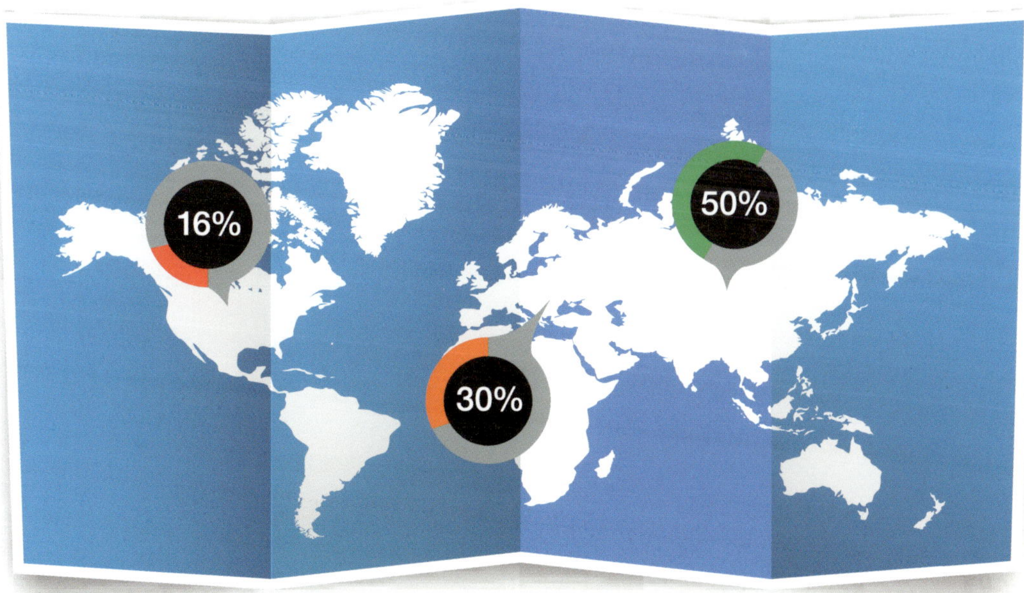

# Comprehension Quiz

**A** Fill in each blank with the right verb below to complete each sentence.

| vacuum | mow | respond | perform |

❶ Some robots ______________ to their environments.

❷ Some robots may ______________ difficult or boring tasks.

❸ Some robots ______________ the floor for their owners.

❹ Some robots can ______________ the lawn.

**B** Circle the right word for each underlined part.

❶ Robots are useful in making small electronic (circuit / curcuit) boards.

❷ Robots are useful in (leesure / leisure) and entertainment.

❸ Some robots can speak and appear to hold a (conversation / conservation).

❹ Robots can be (desined / designed) to play golf, to deal cards, or to play table tennis.

**C** Choose the best answer to each question.

**❶** What do robots do in car factories?

a) They tell the humans what to do.

b) They carry the workers' cell phones.

c) They put together the parts and paint the cars.

d) They design new cars.

**❷** How have chess robots improved over the years?

a) Now they can play golf as well.

b) Now they can move pieces and place them on the board.

c) Now they can play against a human.

d) Now they can design a computer program.

**D** Choose a proper robot for each case.

| domestic robot | roamer | drone | Wakamaru |
| --- | --- | --- | --- |

**❶** to teach a child about angles and distance _______________

**❷** to film someone bungee jumping _______________

**❸** to clean a room _______________

**❹** to guard your house while you are away _______________

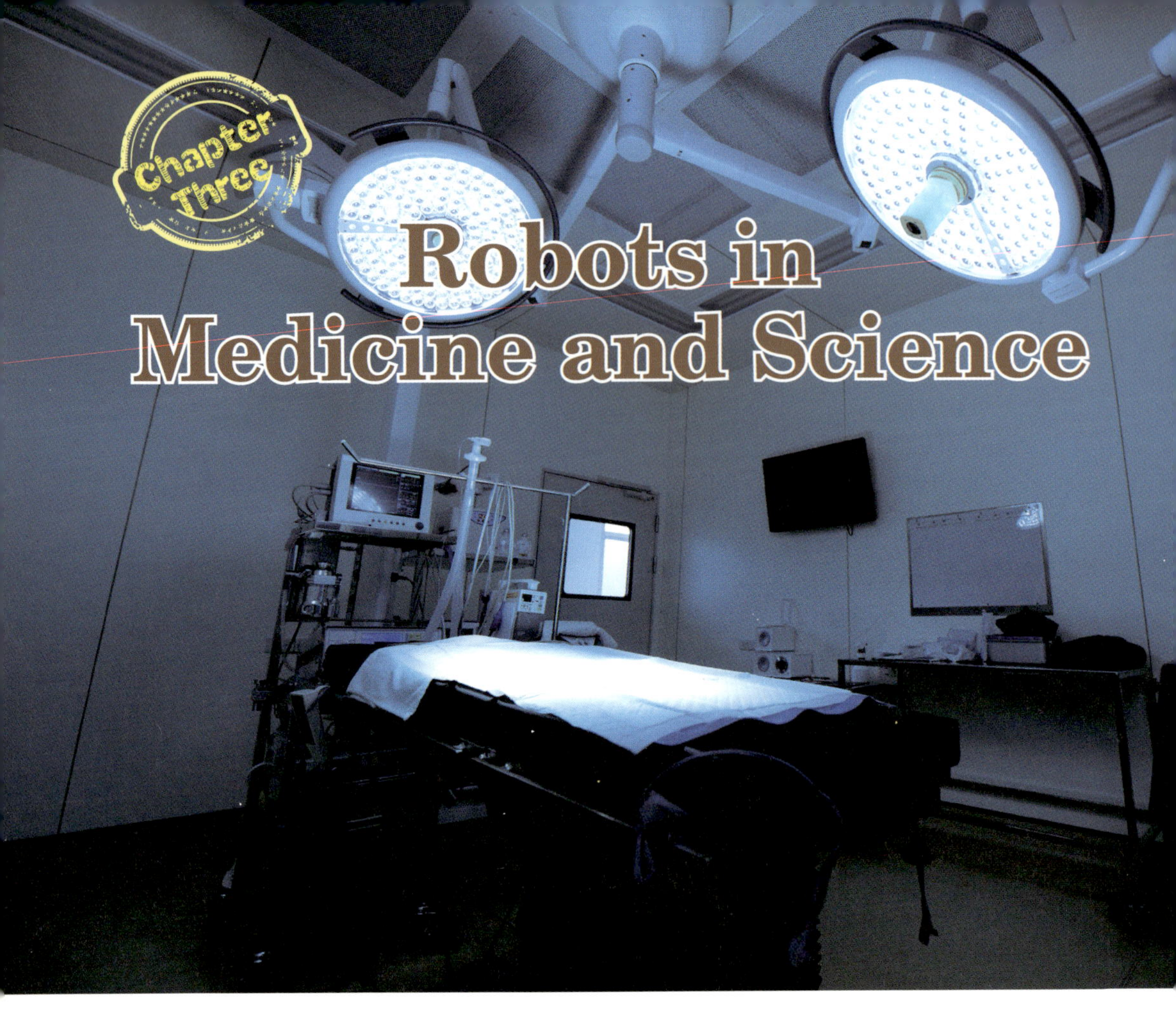


# Robots in Medicine and Science

Since the beginning of the 21st century, robots have been used to perform surgery on humans.

When human surgeons operate, they often need to make a large cut in the patient's body. This gives a good view of the internal organs.

**KEY WORDS**

- medicine
- surgery
- surgeon
- cut
- patient
- give a good view of
- internal
- organ

Surgeons need to use surgical instruments that are the right size for their hands.

However, if these instruments are attached to robotic arms, they can be much smaller. This means that only a small cut needs to be made. This is better for the patient because it means they will heal more quickly.

Also, a camera can be attached to another robotic arm. All these arms can be inside the patient at once. The surgeon has a good view of what is going on.

The surgeon controls the camera and the instruments, but does not have to put his or her hands inside the patient. This reduces the risk of infection, which is another advantage of robotic surgery.

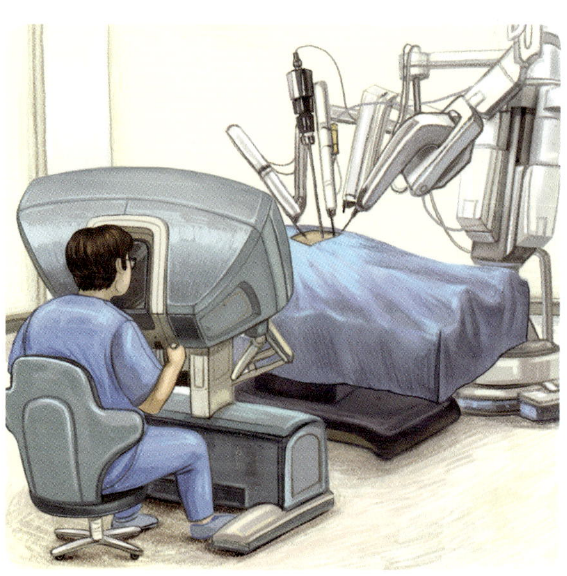

**KEY WORDS**

- surgical
- right
- instrument
- attach

- heal
- at once
- reduce
- risk

- infection
- advantage

In some cases, surgeons may even control the instruments from another room. They look into a 3D monitor that makes them feel as if they were actually inside the patient. The result is that robotic surgery is extremely precise.

The surgeon also remains comfortable and does not get tired so easily. This means that operations lasting several hours become safer for the patient.

**POP QUIZ**

**Which is an advantage of robotic surgery?**
ⓐ It is safer.
ⓑ It is cheaper.

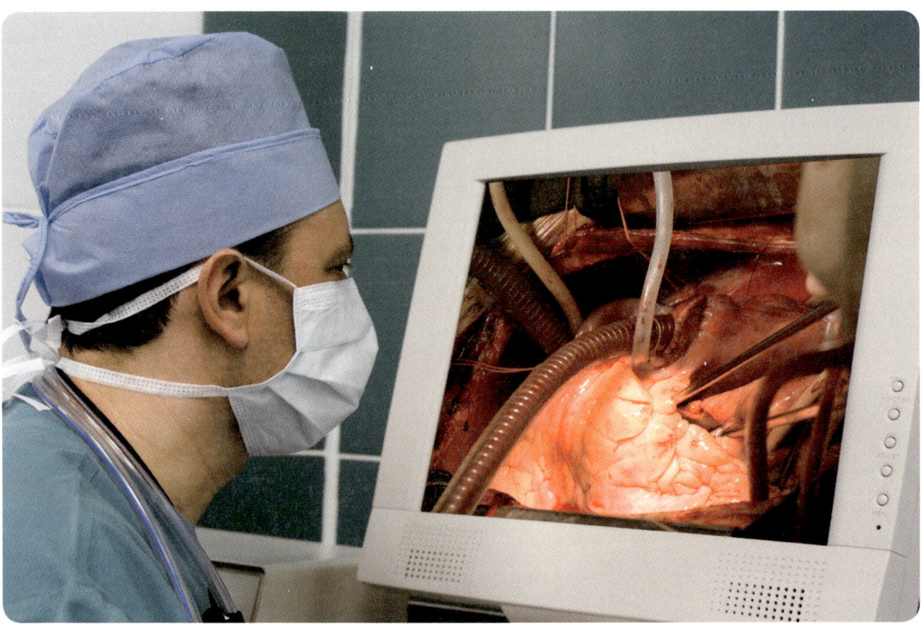

Anesthetics may also be given robotically.

An anesthetic is a drug given to a patient so that they do not feel pain. A general anesthetic also

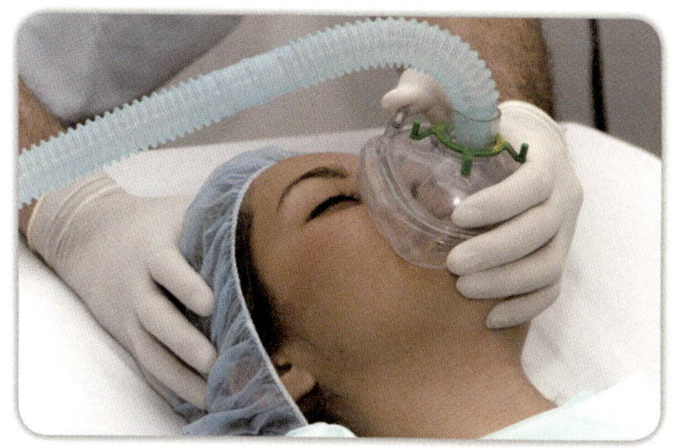

keeps them asleep throughout the surgery. Usually, a human gives the anesthetic. He or she must watch closely to make sure that the right amount of the drug is given. If the patients have too little, they may wake up or suffer a lot of pain. If the patients have too much, it may have a bad effect on their bodies and they may even die.

## KEY WORDS

- in some cases
- **3D** (=3 dimensional)
- monitor
- result
- remain
- last
- anesthetic
- robotically
- drug
- pain

- general
- keep
- throughout
- asleep
- closely
- amount
- **wake up** (wake-woke-woken)
- suffer
- have an effect on

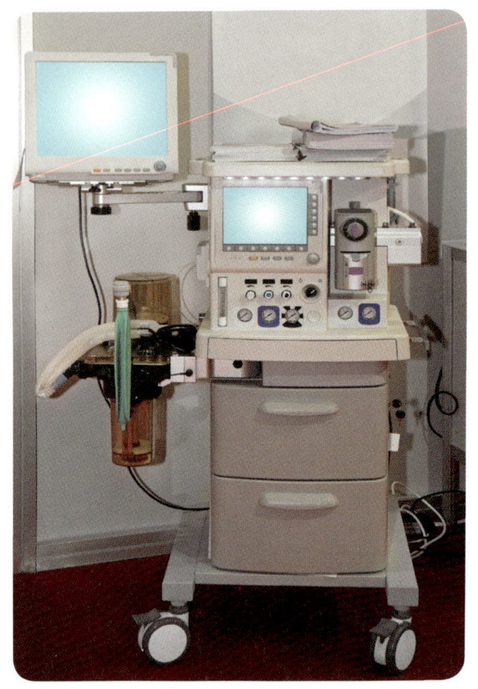

▲ an anesthetic device with a monitor
that shows a patient's condition

Now computer-operated pumps may deliver the anesthetic drug. They may also monitor the patient's body and adjust the dose of the drug.

In 2010, the world's first fully robotic surgery on a human being was carried out in Canada. A human surgeon and a human anesthetist operated their robots. They didn't need to enter the room where the patient lay.

This is still quite rare, but may become more common as technology improves.

**POP QUIZ**

Where did the world's first fully robotic surgery take place?

ⓐ UK
ⓑ Canada

**KEY WORDS**

- deliver
- adjust
- dose

- anesthetist
- lie (lie-lay-lain)
- rare

- common
- improve

Different types of robots are used in other areas of medicine and healthcare. For example, there is a robot that can be attached to a hospital trolley.

It can be programmed to deliver food, dressings or drugs to any part of the hospital when needed. This leaves human staff free to look after the patients, knowing that the delivery robot will bring the things they need.

**KEY WORDS**

- area
- healthcare
- trolley
- dressing
- **leave** (leave-left-left)
- look after
- delivery

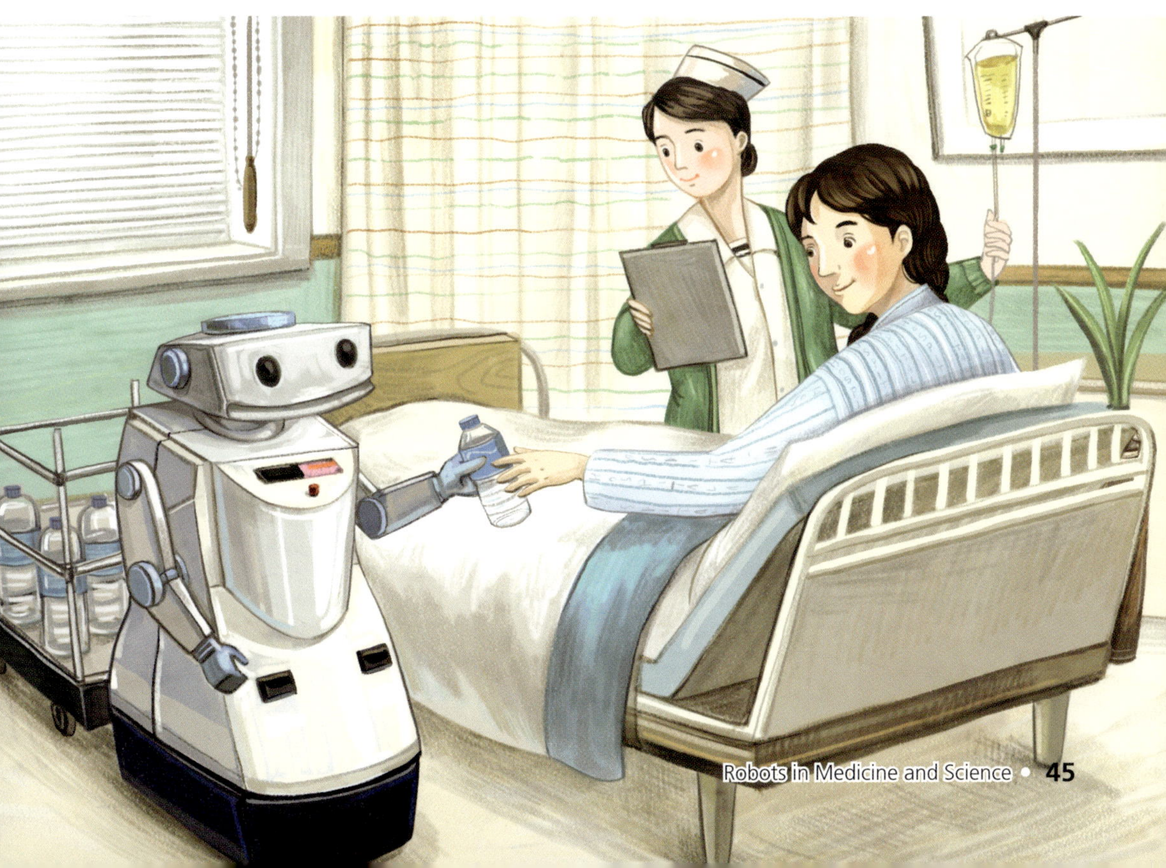

Other robots can record data such as heart rate or blood pressure from a patient. A doctor in another place can check the data and talk about the patient's health with them.

This is particularly useful for patients who may live in remote areas, or who are travelling on an airplane. It is like having a doctor in the room with you. The patient does not need to make a journey to the hospital.

There is even a "robot pill" that is a small capsule around 2 cm long. It is most often used to diagnose intestinal problems. It has a camera, a magnet and a set of mechanical legs.

The patient swallows the robot pill, and it is steered around the intestines using magnets outside the body. Similar robots can be used for cleaning blocked arteries to allow blood to flow properly.

**KEY WORDS**

- heart rate
- blood pressure
- check
- particularly
- remote
- airplane
- make a journey

- pill
- capsule
- diagnose
- intestinal
- magnet
- swallow
- steer

- intestine
- similar
- blocked
- artery
- allow
- flow
- properly

Robots are very useful in places where it is difficult for humans to go. These places include the bottom of the sea, a volcano or outer space.

In 2014, a new underwater robot was produced, which will help scientists study the sea floor. This giant crablike robot, which weighs 635 kg, is called the Crabster. It can move across the sea floor on its mechanical legs, just like a real crab.

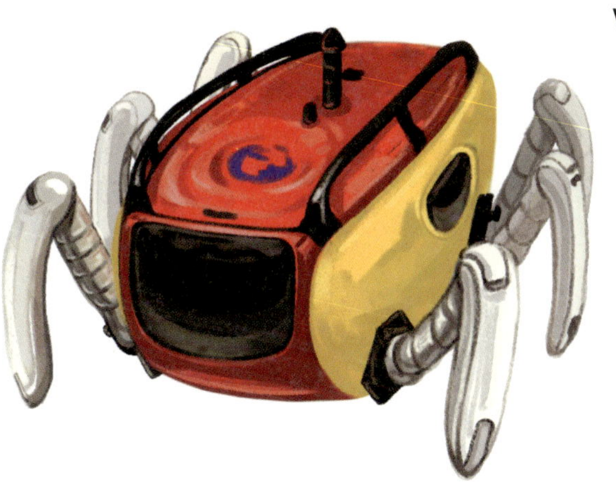



**POP QUIZ**

Where would you find the Crabster?
ⓐ under the sea
ⓑ in intestines

## KEY WORDS

- bottom
- volcano
- outer space
- underwater
- sea floor
- weigh

Similar robots have been used to help scientists explore the deepest parts of the ocean.

Machines that can travel underwater without a human inside are called "robotic submersibles." They are equipped with cameras and are operated from a ship on the surface. They reveal information about sea life and shipwrecks that could never be discovered any other way.

**KEY WORDS**

- explore
- submersible
- be equipped with
- surface
- reveal
- sea life
- shipwreck
- discover

There is even a new underwater robot that may be used to find drugs, weapons or other things that are hidden illegally on board ships.

The robot, which is slightly smaller than a football, is flat on one side and round on the other. The flat side means that it can slide along the outside of a ship. It scans the inside of the ship to see what is being carried. It is a very small, quiet robot, which means that it can do its job secretly.

**KEY WORDS**

- **hide** (hide-hid-hidden)
- **illegally**
- **on board ship**
- slightly
- flat
- slide
- scan
- secretly

Volcanoes are another place where it is dangerous for humans to go. The crater of an erupting volcano is incredibly hot and full of gases. It may also have very steep sides that are difficult for humans to go down.

Robotic instruments can crawl down the sides of a crater and across uneven surfaces. They can withstand the high temperatures of the ground and the air. They sample the air to analyze the gases. They may also be able to pick up samples of rocks.

The data can be sent to scientists who are a safe distance away. They can see what is happening inside the crater without being in any danger.

**What kind of place is a crater?**
ⓐ a dangerous place with no gas
ⓑ a hot place filled with gases

**KEY WORDS**

- crater
- erupting
- incredibly
- steep
- crawl
- uneven
- **withstand** (withstand-withstood-withstood)
- temperature
- sample
- analyze

- be in danger
- astronaut
- spacecraft
- space station
- oxygen
- breathe
- gravity
- in place
- extreme
- spacesuit

Perhaps the most difficult place for humans to go is outer space.
Astronauts can travel in spacecraft or even live on a space
station for a few months. However, it is extremely dangerous for
them to go outside.

There is no oxygen for humans to breathe in space, and
no gravity to hold them in place. They may suffer from the
extremes of heat and cold in space. They can only go outside
their spacecraft in a special spacesuit.

Robots don't have these problems! They don't need to breathe, and they can operate in very hot or cold environments. Robots are also part of a spacecraft. Most spacecraft have several robot arms. They are able to carry out repairs to the outside of the spacecraft. They are operated by astronauts inside the spacecraft.

If there is no gravity, robots can move around easily, even if they are quite large. This means that space robots can be shaped like long snakes. On earth, gravity would pull such a robot down, so that type of robot would break easily.

▲ the unmanned Mars rover, Curiosity

There are also robots in space that are not attached to a spacecraft. Some of them explore the surfaces of planets where people have never been.

NASA has a space program called the Mars Exploration Rover Mission. 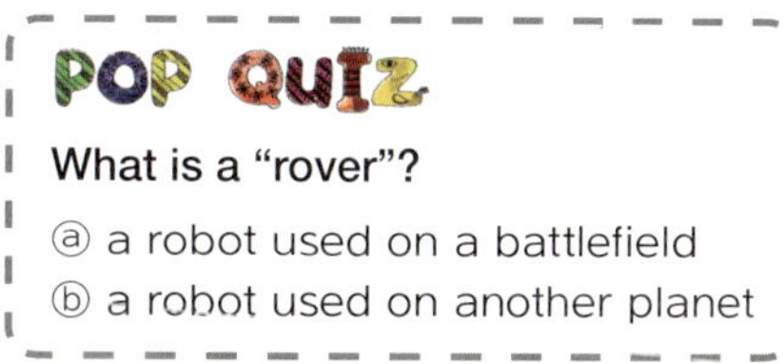 Small robots, called rovers, have been sent to the planet Mars. They will take pictures of the surface and collect data. This information is sent back to scientists on Earth, so that they can learn what Mars is like.



**KEY WORDS**

- repair
- even if
- **break** (break-broke-broken)
- planet
- **NASA** (National Aeronautics and Space Administration)
- rover

On November 12th, 2014, history was made when the robotic probe called Philae landed on a comet. Aha!
A probe is a robot sent out into space to collect data and send it back to Earth.

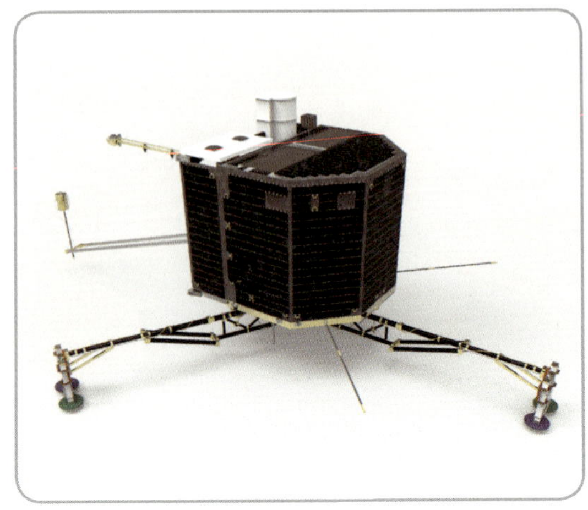

▲ Philae, the robotic probe

Philae is the size of a washing machine and is like a rover, but it does not move about once it has landed.

The probe was transported to the comet on the Rosetta satellite, then launched from there into space. It spent seven hours travelling from the satellite to the comet before landing on it.

## KEY WORDS

- probe
- land
- comet
- transport
- satellite
- launch
- million

- orbit
- at a speed of
- per
- incredible
- manage to + *Verb*
- billion
- catch up to

The comet was 510 million km from Earth when Philae landed on it. But what makes this so amazing is that the comet orbits the sun at speeds of up to 135,000 km per hour.
It is incredible that Philae managed to land on the comet, after travelling over 6 billion km to catch up to it!

▼ the Rosetta satellite and comet 67P/Churyumov-Gerasimenko

▲ A Talon is being operated with a joystick.

Battle zones are very dangerous places for humans to be. For this reason, robots are used in many military operations.

If something goes wrong and a robot is destroyed, only money is lost instead of a human life.

The size and shape of a military robot depend on what type of task it needs to do. Some are the size of trucks. Others can easily be carried by a soldier.

The most common military robot is a small one called the Talon. It travels on tank tracks. It is operated by a soldier using a joystick control, similar to many computer games!

However, this is no game.

**KEY WORDS**

- battle zone
- for this reason
- go wrong
- lose (lose-lost-lost)
- instead of
- depend on
- soldier

- tank
- track
- joystick
- serious
- detect
- chemical
- radiation

- take a photograph
- territory
- machine gun
- grenade launcher
- tough
- amphibious
- equally

Serious operations are carried out by these little robots. They can be used to detect chemicals or radiation. Sometimes, they take photographs of enemy territory using a camera. They may also have machine guns, grenade launchers or other weapons. The Talon is very tough and can travel in very difficult areas. It is also amphibious, which means that it can travel equally well on land or in water!

## POP QUIZ

What is an advantage of having robots in battle zones?
ⓐ They are more economic.
ⓑ They save human lives.

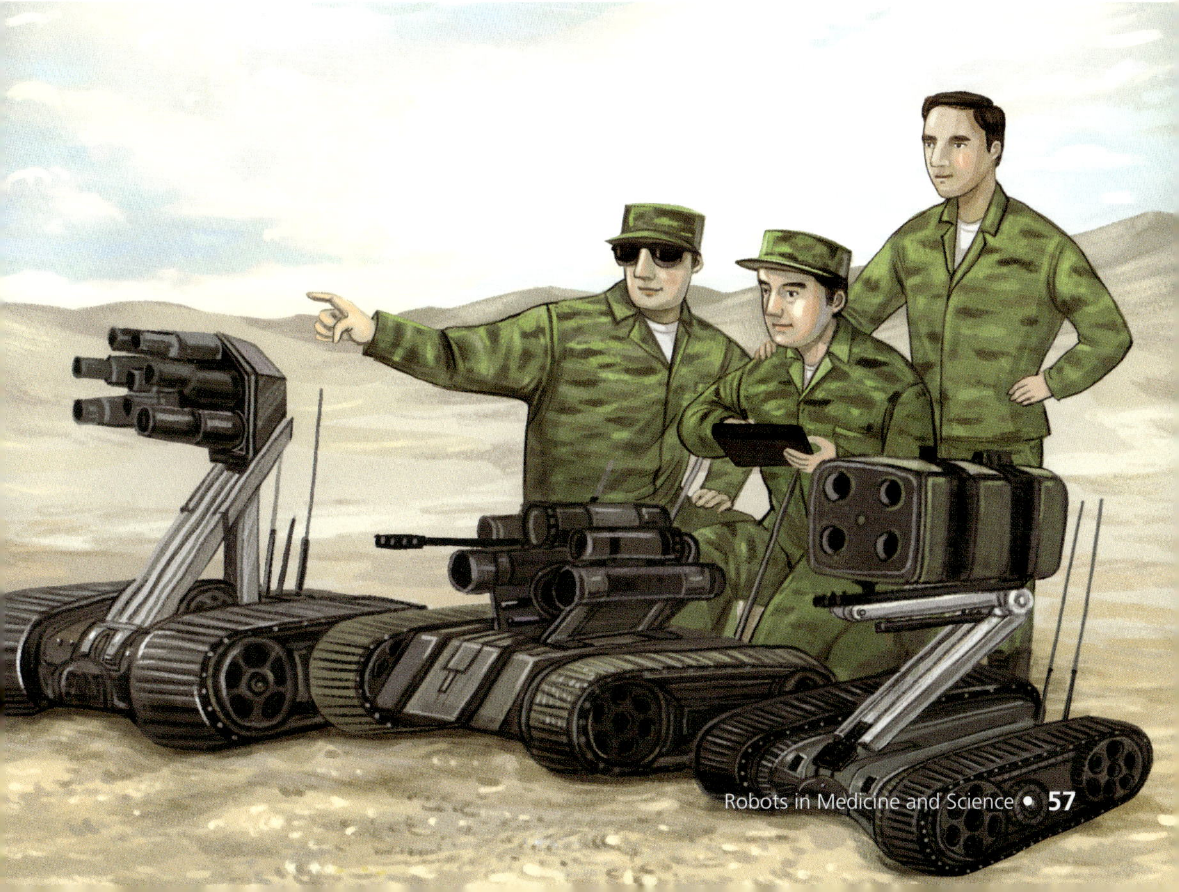

One of the most important uses of military robots is to locate dangerous objects. Then, the robot can remove the objects or destroy them safely.

One of these is the Daksh, a remotely controlled vehicle used for finding bombs. It can climb stairs and use X-rays to see through walls and locate the bombs.

BigDog is a robot that has four legs and moves like a dog. Around 0.9 m long and 0.8 m tall, it can travel over ground that is too difficult for wheels or tank tracks. This means that it can go anywhere with the soldiers. It can carry things for them in places where vehicles cannot go.

BigDog has a computer built into its body. Its legs contain sensors that tell the computer what sort of ground the dog is walking on. They can tell whether it is going up or down a slope. 

Some military robots are basically tanks without human drivers. They look like an armored bulldozer and can carry out heavy lifting tasks. They can rescue overturned vehicles or clear minefields.


**What is special about BigDog?**
ⓐ It can see through walls.
ⓑ It can climb a hill.

**KEY WORDS**

- locate
- remove
- vehicle
- stair
- bomb
- see through

- built into
- sensor
- slope
- basically
- armored
- bulldozer

- lift
- rescue
- overturned
- clear
- minefield

# Chapter Three

# Comprehension Quiz

**A** Choose the right meaning of the given words.

**❶** probe

    a) a robot collecting data in space

    b) a special spacesuit

    c) a robotic cradle

    d) a robot helping cooking

**❷** amphibious

    a) very tough               b) travels on land or in water

    c) takes photographs     d) can detect chemicals

**B** Choose the right word for each underlined part.

**❶** When robotic surgery is used, the (surgeon / patient) does not get tired so easily.

**❷** When robotic surgery is used, the (surgeon / patient) receives very precise treatment.

**❸** When robotic surgery is used, the (surgeon / patient) may control the instruments from another room.

**❹** When robotic surgery is used, the (surgeon / patient) is safer during long operations.

# C   Mark T for true or F for false.

**❶** There is no oxygen in space.     T   F

**❷** It is always cold in space.     T   F

**❸** There is no gravity in space.     T   F

**❹** Robots need spacesuits in space.     T   F


# D   Choose the best two answers to each question.

**❶** Why is robotic surgery better for the patient?

   a) The risk of infection is smaller.

   b) The surgery is painless.

   c) A smaller cut can be made in the body.

   d) A robot surgeon is more intelligent than a human surgeon.

**❷** Why is it important that exactly the right dose of anesthetic is given?

   a) If there is too little anesthetic, the patient may not wake up.

   b) If there is too much anesthetic, the patient may not wake up.

   c) If there is too little anesthetic, the patient may wake up too soon.

   d) If there is too much anesthetic, the patient may wake up too soon.

Chapter Four

# The Future of Robots

Robots have captured the imagination of many people. New robots are being developed all the time.

Perhaps the most advanced humanoid robot is ASIMO. This stands for Advanced Step in Innovative Mobility. This Japanese robot moves like a human and is the size of a small adult.

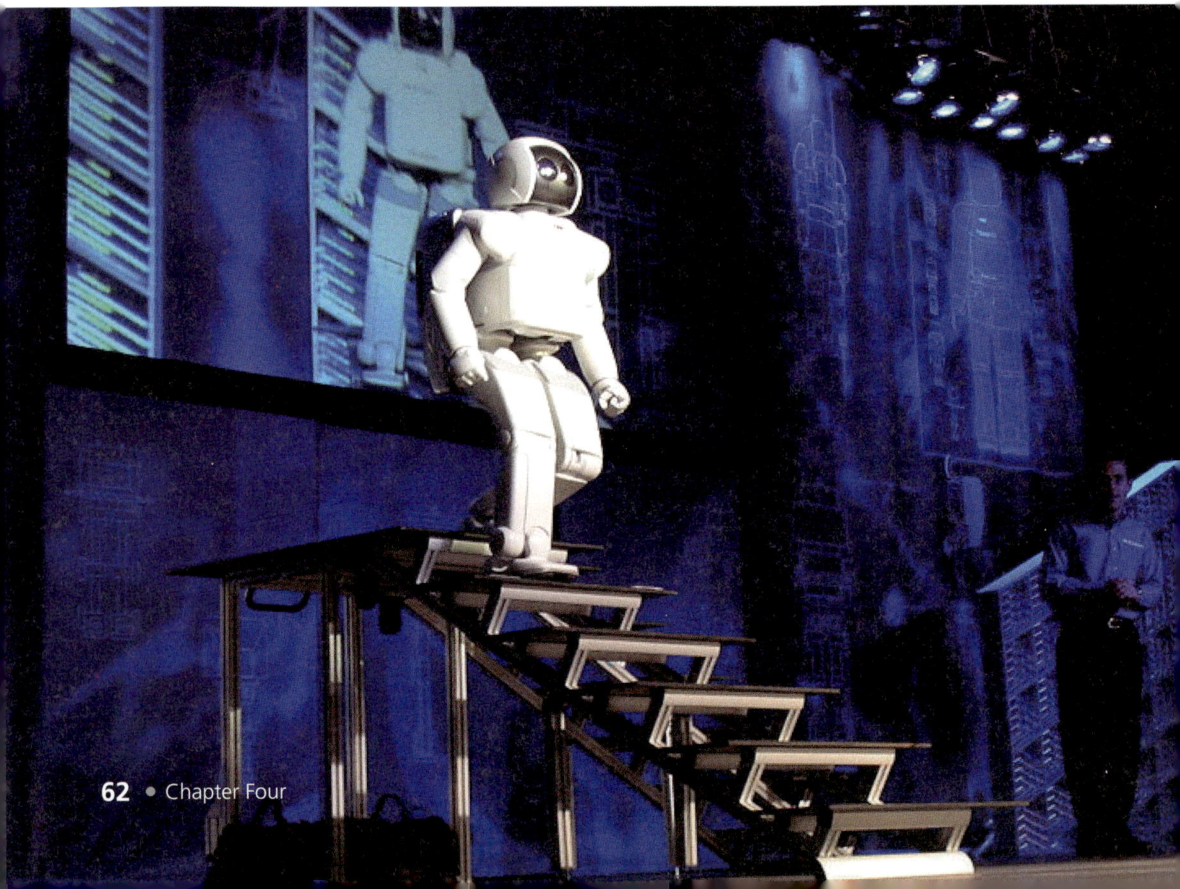

▲ (By Satoru Fujiwara (IMGP1760) [CC BY 2.0 (http://creativecommons.org/licenses/by/2.0)], via Wikimedia Commons)

It can walk and run quickly, both forwards and backwards. It can go up and down stairs, hop, and jump.

It can also kick a football into a goal, wave its hands and hold a conversation. It can respond to humans nearby by turning towards them and offering food or water.

In the future, ASIMO's creators hope that it will be able to help people in many different ways. Perhaps many homeowners in the future will have a robot like this to serve their needs.

**What can ASIMO do?**
ⓐ It can talk with people.
ⓑ It can fly in the air.

**KEY WORDS**

- capture
- develop
- advanced
- humanoid
- stand for
- innovative

- mobility
- adult
- hop
- goal
- wave
- nearby

- turn
- offer
- creator
- homeowner
- serve
- need

A similar robot for use in the home is the South Korean robot called CIROS. It is able to pick up a knife, hold onto vegetables, and chop them to make a salad. It is much slower than a human, but as technology develops it could replace human cooks in the kitchen.

This raises a question that concerns many people.

With more robots doing jobs, will there be fewer jobs for humans to do?

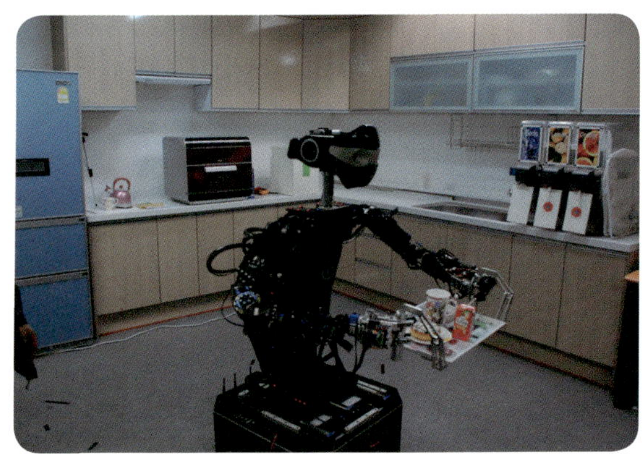

▲ CIROS
(by Center for Intelligent Robotics (http://irobotics.re.kr))

## KEY WORDS

- for use
- hold onto
- chop
- cook
- raise a question
- concern
- checkout

- **withdraw** (withdraw-withdrew-withdrawn)
- **pay** (pay-paid-paid)
- in order to + *Verb*
- argue
- therefore
- enough
- support

Already, robots are used in factories. Self-service checkouts are common in supermarkets. Money can be withdrawn from machines.

Humans need jobs that pay them money in order to live. Some people argue that the greater use of robots may mean fewer jobs for humans. Therefore people will not have enough money to support themselves and their families.



**Where would you find a self-service checkout?**
ⓐ in a supermarket
ⓑ in a factory

The advantages of using robots are clear. They don't need to be paid and they can work long hours, sometimes without stopping at all. They don't complain about working conditions or require rest breaks. They are efficient and make fewer mistakes. However, humans are better at adapting to different situations. They can recognize emotions in other people more easily than a robot can. This is important in caring jobs such as medicine. Many people prefer talking to a real human being rather than to a machine or a robot. They also fear that a robot may become uncontrollable.



## KEY WORDS

- complain about
- condition
- require
- rest break
- efficient
- make a mistake
- be better at

- adapt
- situation
- emotion
- prefer
- fear
- uncontrollable

There has been a lot of discussion in the UK about "driverless cars." These vehicles are operated by a computer. They use satellite technology to drive along pre-programmed routes. They follow instructions about where to go.

Driverless cars respond to problems on the road such as traffic accidents. 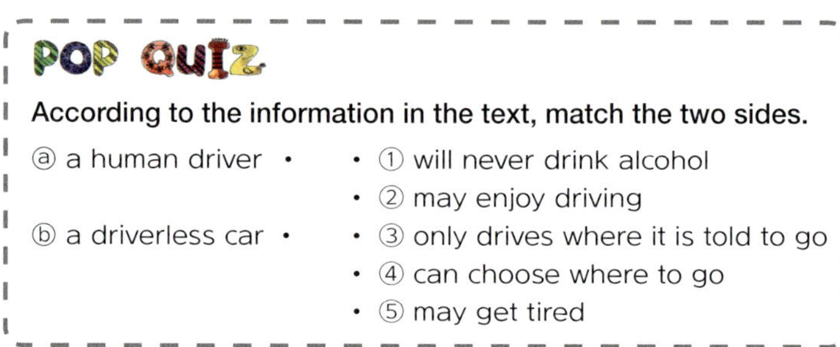 They know when to stop, turn or slow down. The developers hope that these cars might reduce the number of traffic accidents.

The cars would not get tired or be distracted. They would not drink alcohol or be affected by emotions.

But some people do not like the idea of driverless cars. They fear that the car may not respond quickly enough in an emergency. They worry that it may take them where they do not want to go. Many people enjoy driving a car and being in control of it.

## POP QUIZ

According to the information in the text, match the two sides.

ⓐ a human driver •

ⓑ a driverless car •

• ① will never drink alcohol
• ② may enjoy driving
• ③ only drives where it is told to go
• ④ can choose where to go
• ⑤ may get tired

**KEY WORDS**

- traffic accident
- slow down
- be affected

- emergency
- be in control of (↔ lose control of)

This is another issue that concerns people. Will robots take over
the world?

Humans do not want to lose control of robots. However, some
robots are being developed that appear to think for themselves.
They operate without humans controlling them.

**KEY WORDS**

- issue
- take over

- for oneself

One example is the "Kilobot" swarm revealed by Harvard University in 2014.

The Kilobots are a group of more than a thousand tiny robots. They work together by sensing and responding to each other. They behave in a similar way to natural creatures that work in large groups, such as bees or termites.

If a simple command is given to form a shape, the Kilobots carry this out by working together. The ones on the outside of the group move to their places, and then the others follow.

For now, they only make simple shapes. But the technology could be used to make larger robots that work together as one group.

▲ (By asuscreative (Own work) [CC BY-SA 4.0 (http://creativecommons.org/licenses/by-sa/4.0)], via Wikimedia Commons)

**KEY WORDS**

- swarm
- creature
- termite
- form
- for now

Instead of making bigger robots, some experts are making the smallest possible robots, called nanobots. "Nano" means a measurement that is one billionth of a meter. 

A robot like this would be no bigger than a few atoms. They may have many medical uses, since they could be put into the human body and travel about body systems. They could deliver drugs anywhere in the body, or collect data to inform doctors.

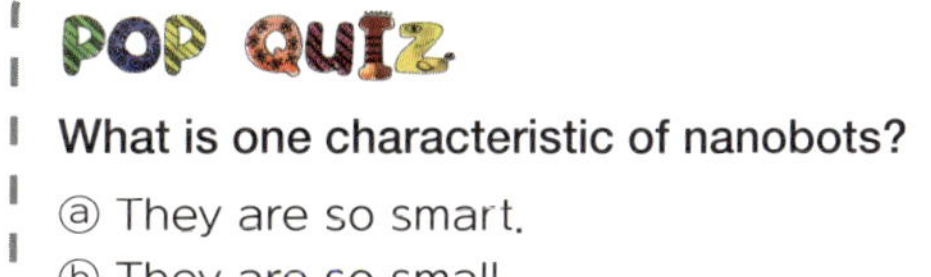


**What is one characteristic of nanobots?**

ⓐ They are so smart.
ⓑ They are so small.

**KEY WORDS**

- expert
- nanobot
- measurement

- atom
- inform

Some scientists hope that nanobots may be used to cure cancer.

The cells that cause a cancer tumor to grow must be removed or destroyed without damaging healthy cells. So far, this has been very difficult to do.

Many cancer treatments destroy healthy cells as well. The effects of the treatment are very unpleasant for the patient.

The "bad" cells that cause cancer occur because of a fault that occurs in a person's DNA. If nanobots can cut out faulty parts of the DNA, then the cancer will not develop.

It sounds like a good plan, but the human body may fight the nanobots. It knows that they come from outside the body and shouldn't be there. 

The patient might destroy something that would help in fighting the cancer! So a lot more research is required.

**KEY WORDS**

- cure
- cancer
- cell
- cause
- tumor
- **grow** (grow-grew-grown)
- damage
- healthy
- so far

- treatment
- as well
- unpleasant
- occur
- because of
- **fault** (*cf.* faulty)
- **DNA** (deoxyribonucleic acid)
- sound like
- research

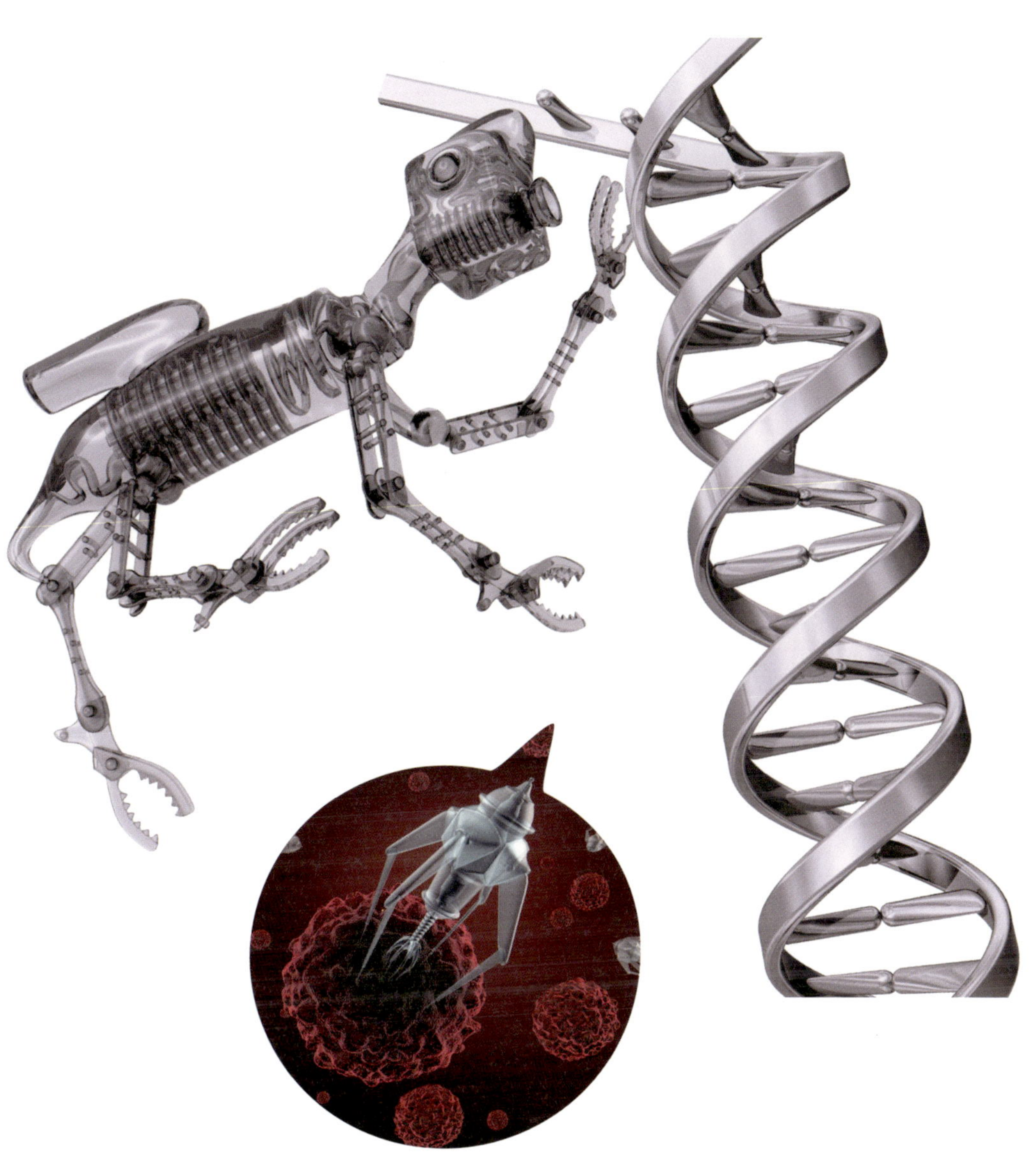

▲ It is expected that nanobots will be used to cut out faulty parts of human DNA to prevent developing cancer in the future.

Some people dream of other uses for nanobots. They believe that nanobots will one day be used to replace human organs. Then, we will become partly robotic ourselves.

They hope that nanobots in the brain will allow humans to replay data like a computer or DVD player can. They believe that in the future, human brains could be directly connected to the computer "cloud." This is a virtual computer network for storing data and finding it again.

Imagine that! You would be taking an exam and it would be like having the entire Internet in your mind. You could retrieve any piece of information you wanted, simply with a thought.

Ideas like this may remain science fiction, but what if they were to become fact?

Human life would be completely different than it is now.

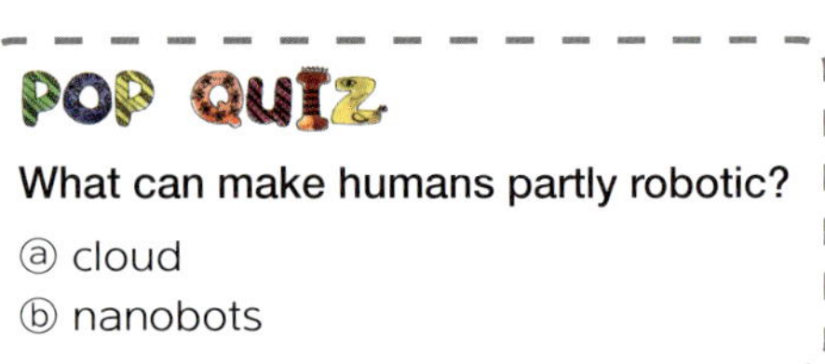

## KEY WORDS

- brain
- replay
- directly
- connect
- network
- store
- take an exam
- entire
- mind
- retrieve
- thought
- What if ~?
- fact
- completely
- different than

And some people say that, one day, nanobots will be everywhere. They will be in our clothes, in our bodies, and in the environment around us. We will have no choice but to interact with them.

Many people do not want a future like this. They believe that freedom of choice is the right of every human.

Scientists are also developing robots that can learn. French scientists have developed a one-meter tall childlike robot called the iCub. 

The iCub can learn new languages in the same way that a human does. It listens to instructions and repeats them to be sure that they are correct. Then, it "thinks" about the meaning.

Of course, a robot cannot truly think for itself, but it can be programmed to recognize words and link them to actions. After some "thinking" time, the robot carries out the instructions. Each time this is done correctly, the robot is learning something new. Technology is developing all the time. New and better robots will be developed each year.

But what effects will they have on the human race? Do you think that having more robots in the world is a good thing, or a bad thing? Whatever you think, robots are here to stay.



**KEY WORDS**

- **have no choice but to** (= cannot help + Verb-ing) (*cf.* choice)
- **interact with**
- **freedom**
- **link A to B**
- **race**
- **whatever**
- **be here to stay**

# Comprehension Quiz

**A** Match each robot with the right description.

❶ nanobot  ·   ·  a) It can "learn" new things.

❷ Kilobot  ·   ·  b) It is one billionth of a meter long.

❸ ASIMO  ·   ·  c) It works in groups.

❹ iCub  ·   ·  d) It is a Japanese robot.

**B** Mark T for true or F for false.

❶ Nanobots could help us to pass exams.   **T F**

❷ The "bad" cells that cause cancer occur because of a fault that occurs in Nanobots.   **T F**

❸ Nanobots could replace diseased organs.   **T F**

❹ We could find data just by thinking about it.   **T F**

**C** Choose the best answer to each question.

❶ Why are some people concerned about robots doing their jobs?

a) They think that robots might destroy humans.

b) They think that robots cannot do the job as well as they can.

c) They think that robots will take all the jobs, so that humans will not be able to make money.

d) They think that robots should only be seen in movies.

❷ Why are humans better than robots at some medical jobs?

a) They are efficient and do not make mistakes.

b) They can work long hours without stopping.

c) They can recognize emotions in other people.

d) They do not become uncontrollable.

**D** Rearrange the following sentences according to the order that iCub learns new things.

❶ The iCub repeats the instructions to be sure that they are correct.

❷ The iCub carries out the instructions.

❸ The iCub listens to some instructions.

❹ The iCub "thinks" about the meaning of the instructions.

________ → ________ → ________ → ________

# Let's Review the Story

Fill in the blanks to review the story.

Title: All about ________

**Chapter 1:**
- A robot is a m________ that carries out actions in response to a p________ or a c________.
- Robotic technology has advanced through the years, from a wooden bird to robots that use a________ intelligence.

**Chapter 2:**
- D________ robots do many useful jobs in our homes.
- Educational and l________ robots t________ and entertain us.
- Robots make many things in f________.

**Chapter 3:**
- Robots can make surgery ________ and more precise.
- Robots can go to places that humans can't, e.g. under the s________, into a v________, or into s________.
- M________ robots are used to help soldiers in b________ and to keep them safe.

**Chapter 4:**
- Robots will h________ humans every day by doing many helpful tasks that h________ do now, e.g. driving a car or cooking.
- ________ may be used to prevent cancer or to replace human ________.
- Now some ________ can "l________," so they might have the ability to "t________" to a great degree in the future.

# Let's Think & Talk

**Think about the following questions and answer them freely.**

❶ Among the robots in the book, which robot do you think helps humans the most and why?

❷ Will robots do all the work for humans someday? If all the employees in restaurants and shops are robots, what convenience or discomfort will there be?

❸ If some parts of the human body are robotized, what will happen? Would you agree or disagree to insert a robot into your body? Tell us the reason why or why not.

❹ If technology is more developed someday, will robots have emotions? Will robots be able to love other robots or humans like humans do? If it actually happens, what are the pros and cons?

# Let's Review the Story

Title: All about **Robots**

**Chapter 1:**
- A robot is a **machine** that carries out actions in response to a **program** or a **command**.
- Robotic technology has advanced through the years, from a wooden bird to robots that use **artificial** intelligence.

**Chapter 2:**
- **Domestic** robots do many useful jobs in our homes.
- Educational and **leisure** robots **teach** and entertain us.
- Robots make many things in **factories**.

**Chapter 3:**
- Robots can make surgery **safer** and more precise.
- Robots can go to places that humans can't, e.g. under the **sea**, into a **volcano**, or into **space**.
- **Military** robots are used to help soldiers in **battle** and to keep them safe.

**Chapter 4:**
- Robots will **help** humans every day by doing many helpful tasks that **humans** do now, e.g. driving a car or cooking.
- **Nanobots** may be used to prevent cancer or to replace human **organs**.
- Now some **robots** can "**learn**," so they might have the ability to "**think**" to a great degree in the future.

- All about Robots
- Level 5
- 27 Questions

  (Vocabulary 6 / Reading Comprehension 16 /

  Sentence Structure & Grammar 5)

1. What is a "domestic" robot?
   ① a robot that can be programmed
   ② a robot that does not think for itself
   ③ a robot that can hold a conversation
   ④ a robot that is used in the home

2. What does "animatronic" mean?
   ① expensive, but educational
   ② robotic, but lifelike
   ③ playful, but frightening
   ④ cheap, but fun

3. Which of the following words has the wrong opposite?
   ① distract ↔ detect               ② unusual ↔ usual
   ③ forwards ↔ backwards            ④ be in use ↔ be out of use

4. What does "driverless" mean?
   ① without a driver               ② with an extra driver
   ③ easier to drive                ④ more difficult to drive

5. Choose the right word for the blank.

   > In 2010, the world's first fully robotic __________ on a human being was carried out in Canada.

   ① surgeon                        ② surface
   ③ surround                       ④ surgery

6. What is the common word for the two blanks?

> • It was made of wood and powered ___________ steam.
> • The first remote control device was a boat, invented __________ Nikola Tesla in 1898.

① on                          ② by
③ for                         ④ with


7. Why did Magnus' student smash the brass man?
   ① It frightened him.
   ② It talked too much.
   ③ It asked him questions.
   ④ It hurt his servant.


8. Isaac Asimov was the first person to use the word "___________."
   ① remote control              ② machines
   ③ robotics                    ④ intelligence


9. Why can we consider a TV to be a robot?
   ① It shows human faces on its screen.
   ② It has flashing lights.
   ③ It responds to a command or program.
   ④ It operates by using electricity.


10. Why do people buy a companion robot?
    ① They want to give it as a gift to a friend.
    ② They want it to help them write emails.
    ③ They want it to go to work instead of them.
    ④ They want to feel like having a friend with them.

11. What is a "roamer"?
    ① a special pen that helps a child to learn how to read
    ② a robot that is used in a factory to make car parts
    ③ a robotic arm that repeats the same movement over and over again
    ④ an educational device that moves about on the floor in response to
       computer instructions


12. Why are robots better than humans at working in factories? Choose two
    answers.
    ① They never get tired or distracted.
    ② They cost nothing to run.
    ③ They understand their task better.
    ④ They can repeat precisely the same movement.


13. Which continent has around half of the world's robots?
    ① North America              ② Europe
    ③ South America              ④ Asia


14. Where would you use a "robotic submersible"?
    ① in a volcano               ② under the sea
    ③ in space                   ④ on a battlefield


15. What is the most important reason to use robots on the battlefield?
    ① They can fight better than humans can.
    ② They can travel over different types of ground.
    ③ Fewer human lives may be lost.
    ④ Robots can see through walls.

16. According to the text, which task can an armored bulldozer NOT do?
    ① use X-rays to see through walls
    ② lift heavy objects
    ③ rescue overturned vehicles
    ④ clear minefields

17. Why is CIROS NOT yet better than a human at making a salad?
    ① It cannot hold a knife.
    ② It cannot work quickly.
    ③ It cannot hold onto vegetables.
    ④ It cannot chop foods.

18. How big is a nanobot?
    ① the size of one atom
    ② one billionth of a meter long
    ③ one kilometer long
    ④ two centimeters long

19. Why are many cancer treatments NOT good for the patient?
    ① They do not work.
    ② They cause tumors to grow.
    ③ They damage the patient's DNA.
    ④ They destroy healthy cells as well as cancer cells.

20. How might nanobots help in the fight against cancer?
    ① They will make the patients unpleasant.
    ② They will help the cancer tumor grow.
    ③ They will prevent the cancer from beginning.
    ④ They will replace cancer tumors.

21. What problem might occur in the use of nanobots to fight diseases?
① The disease might destroy the nanobots.
② The human body might fight against the nanobots.
③ The nanobots might get lost inside the patient.
④ The patient might not allow the doctor to put nanobots into his/her body.

22. What is special about the iCub, that is not true of any other robot?
① It looks like a child.
② It responds to instructions.
③ It can speak.
④ It can "learn" new things.

※ Choose the wrong part of each sentence. (23~24)

23.
It's full-sized and looks really.
　① 　　　② 　　　　　③ 　　④

24.
"Nano" means a measurement that is first billionth of a meter.
　　　　① 　　　　　　　　　② 　　③ 　　④

※ Choose the correct sentence. (25~26)
25. ① But the real world of robots is far wider than this.
② But the real world of robots is wide far than this.
③ But the real world of robots is far wide than this.
④ But the real world of robots is wider far than this.

**26.** ① He must watch closely to make sure to the right amount of the drug is given.

② He must watch closely to make sure that the right amount of the drug is receive.

③ He must watch closely to make sure that the right amount of the drug is given.

④ He must watch closely to make sure to the right amount of the drug receive.


**27.** Choose the correct word for the blank.

> The more robots there are in a factory, the _____________ humans are needed to do the work.

① few                                     ② fewer
③ little                                   ④ smaller

# Memo

# Memo 

 Memo

# Memo

**Sarah J. Dodd**

Sarah J. Dodd is an experienced primary school teacher who resides in the UK, but has also lived and taught in Australia. She has a PhD in Science and a certificate in Creative Writing. She has published several books for children: "An Angel Anyway" (Anyway Press, 2008) the "Little Angels" series (Lion Children's Books, 2009/10), "The Lion Picture Bible" (Lion Children's Books, 2015) and "Legs: the tale of a meerkat lost and found" (Lion Children's Books, 2015). Her poetry for children has also been highly commended and published in the anthology "Let in the Stars" (Manchester Metropolitan University, 2014).
She is currently working on further picture books for the very young, and a novel for older children.

# All about Robots

Written by Sarah J. Dodd
Illustrated by Dahye Choi

First Published in December 2015

Editorial Manager: Juyon Choi
Editors: Juyon Choi, Myungjin Kim, Kyunghee Jang, Jiyeong Park
Designers: Eunhee Lee, Elim
Cover Designer: Eunhee Lee

Published and distributed by

Darakwon Bldg., 64-1 Jandari-ro, Mapo-gu, Seoul, Korea 04031
Tel: 82-2-736-2031(ext. 250)     Fax: 82-2-732-2037
Homepage: www.ihappyhouse.co.kr
Publisher: Kyudo Chung



ISBN: 978-89-6653-215-5 18740 / 978-89-6653-156-1 18740(set)

[Components]
• 1 Audio CD (Recording Studio: Aram)
• Answer Keys & Korean Translation: Free download at www.ihappyhouse.co.kr